How to Defeat Dragons

How to Defeat DRaGonS

Catherine Leblanc   Roland Garrigue

INSIGHT KIDS

San Rafael, California

You've probably never defeated a dragon....

But you'd better be ready in case one shows up on your street corner!
Dragons are mythical creatures that fly around and breathe fire.

DRAGON

bat

lizard

snake

they fly

they spit fire

Their crocodile heads can terrify you, and so can their snakelike bodies,
their big bat wings, their creepy lizard tails, their giant eagle claws,
and their sharp lion teeth. They have many, many powers from unknown worlds.

ram

lion

crocodile

eagle

It's oh so very hard to stop them!
So protect yourself with a mirror shield.
That way, you'll be able to reflect the
rays of the sun into the dragon's eyes.
This will make it blind, and it will start
flying sideways, unable to catch you.

how to defeat one:

sun

dragon

mirror
shield

me

Even if you hide out in your room, a dragon can s t r e t c h its very long neck through your window. Its nostrils will smoke, its breath will smell like rotten eggs, and its eyes will try to hypnotize you.

Gather all your strength and courage and cut off its head!

And if you see more than one head,
start juggling a chicken at full speed
and watch as those dragon necks
get all tangled up!

Thankfully,
dragons like to hibernate
deep inside their caves.
Take advantage of their long slumber
to tie up all their feet.

When they wake up,
they'll see who the clever one is.

The hardest ones to find and catch are the tiny little dragons.
They can hide out almost anywhere. They are great at making messes at your school.
They like to fly from classroom to classroom, scorching the toes of the children,
burning all their notebooks, and frying the teacher's hair.

Catch them with a net!
Once they're locked in a tank,
it's time to study them.

Some dragons live deep in lakes. They like to pop out of the water and make enormous *waves*.

Don't get washed away! Hurry to the shore and put on your scary rhino costume. This will frighten the dragon, which will dive deep under water and leave you alone.

The most terrifying dragon of all is a huge beast that can wrap itself
around an entire skyscraper and squeeze it to the ground.
Not even an entire fleet of helicopters can defeat it. But here's the secret!
Say this magic spell to make the dragon vanish:

Rabracabrada!
Abracadragongo!

Be very careful! Even if you don't see any more dragons around you,
one is probably hidden somewhere. . . .

Be sure to locate all the eggs before they hatch.

Cook them into a giant omelet.

Eat it, and you'll be able to breathe fire!

You can also choose to keep
one of the eggs,

and raise a little dragon
as your pet.

If you teach your dragon well, no harm will ever come to you.
In fact, you'll have a permanent bodyguard!

The End

Catherine Leblanc

lives in Angers, France, where she was born.
A trained psychologist, she writes novels
and poems for children and adults.

To Louane, to help you catch those
dragon-butterflies. —CL

Roland Garrigue

lives in Paris and specializes in illustration
for young readers. He searched far and wide
in order to create the frightening sketches
of abominable creatures for this series.

To Simon, the little
dragon of Viroflay. —RG

INSIGHT
KIDS

PO Box 3088
San Rafael, CA 94912
www.insighteditions.com

Find us on Facebook: www.facebook.com/InsightEditions
Follow us on Twitter: @insighteditions

First published in hardcover in the United States by Insight Editions
in 2014, and subsequently in paperback by Insight Editions in 2014.
Originally published in France in 2012 by Éditions Glénat as
Comment Ratatiner les Dragons? by C. Leblanc and R. Garrigue.
© 2012 Éditions Glénat. Translation © 2014 Insight Editions.

Thanks to Christopher Goff and Marie Goff-Tuttle
for their help in translating this book.

Library of Congress Cataloging-in-Publication Data available.

ISBN: 978-1-60887-412-5

ROOTS of PEACE   ⊕REPLANTED PAPER

Insight Editions, in association with Roots of Peace, will plant two trees for each tree used in the
manufacturing of this book. Roots of Peace is an internationally renowned humanitarian organization
dedicated to eradicating land mines worldwide and converting war-torn lands into productive farms
and wildlife habitats. Roots of Peace will plant two million fruit and nut trees in Afghanistan and
provide farmers there with the skills and support necessary for sustainable land use.

Manufactured in China by Insight Editions

10 9 8 7 6 5 4 3 2 1